E
UNG

Ungerer, Tomi,
1931-

Crictor.

$13.89

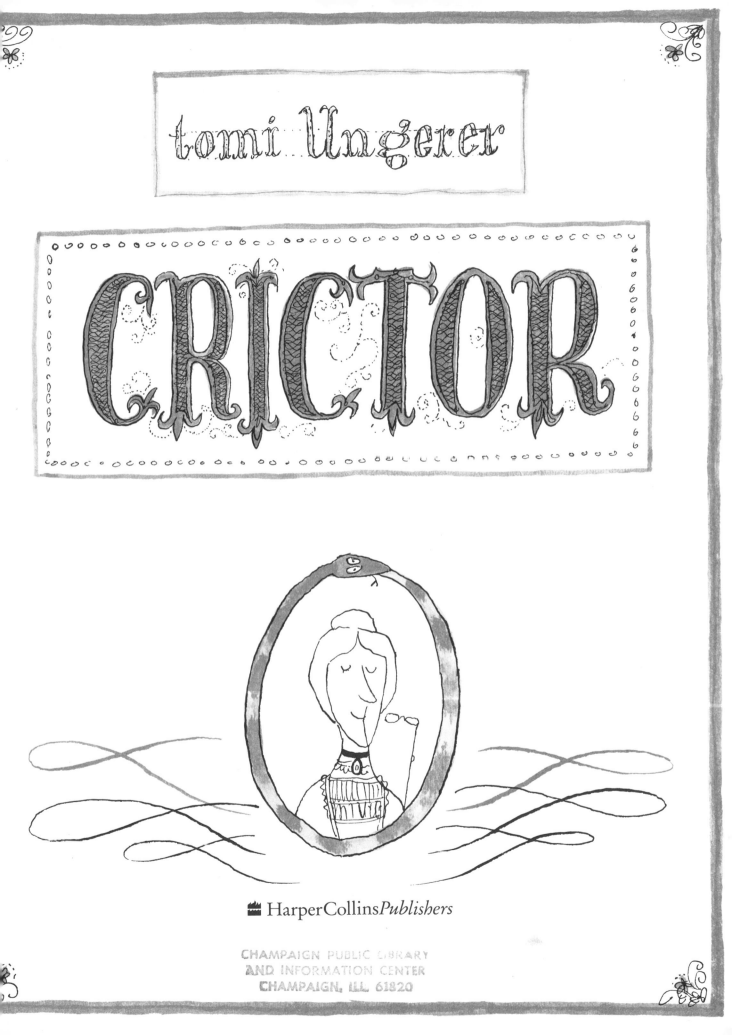

tomi Ungerer

CRICTOR

HarperCollins*Publishers*

For Nancy, Ursula and Susan

CRICTOR
Copyright © 1958 by Jean Thomas Ungerer
Copyright renewed 1986 by Tomi Ungerer
All rights in this book are reserved.
Printed in Mexico.

Library of Congress Catalog Card Number: 58-5288
ISBN 0-06-026180-3
ISBN 0-06-026181-1 (lib. bdg.)
ISBN 0-06-443044-8 (pbk.)

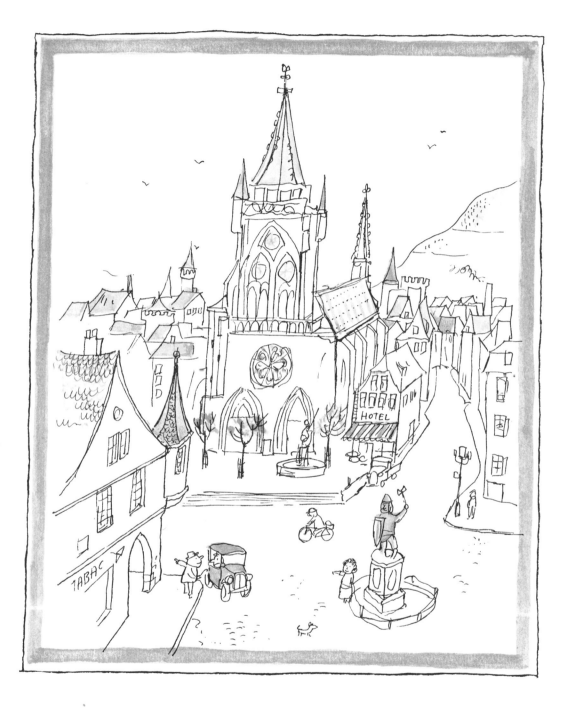

Once upon a time in a little French town

4   lived an old lady whose name was Madame Louise Bodot.

She had one son who was in Africa studying reptiles.

One morning the mailman brought her a peculiar O-shaped box.

Madame Bodot screamed when she opened it.

It was a snake her son had sent her for her birthday.

To make sure it was not a poisonous snake, she went to the zoo.
She identified it as a boa constrictor. So she called her animal
Crictor.

Madame Bodot mothered her new pet, feeding it bottles of milk.

She bought palm trees so Crictor would really feel at home.

As dogs do when they are happy, he wagged his tail.

Well fed, Crictor grew longer and longer and stronger and stronger.   11

The boa followed his mistress when she went shopping.

Everyone was astonished.

Madame Bodot knitted a long woolen sweater
for her pet to wear on cold days.

Crictor also had a warm, comfortable bed.

There he would dream happily, under his palm trees. 15

16   In the winter it was fun for Crictor to wriggle in the snow.

Madame Bodot taught at the public school.

One day she decided to take Crictor to her classes.

He could count too, forming figures.

 for your two hands

for the three little pigs

for the four legs of the dog

for your five fingers

for the six legs of a bug

for the seven dwarfs

for the eight arms of the octopus

The boa liked to play with little boys

and little girls too.

He helped the boy scouts learn knots.

Crictor was a helpful snake. 25

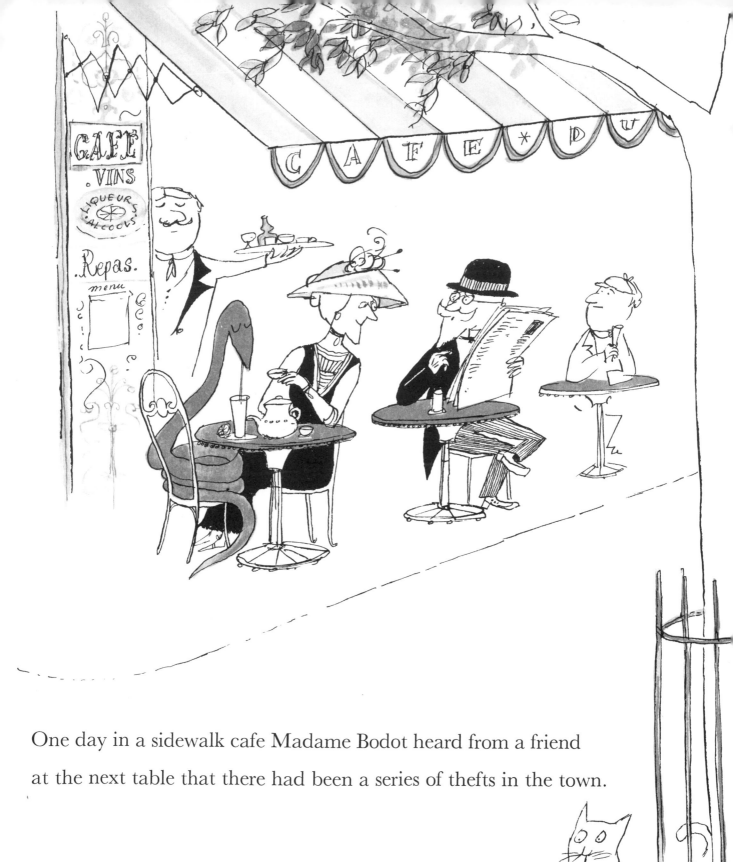

One day in a sidewalk cafe Madame Bodot heard from a friend
at the next table that there had been a series of thefts in the town.

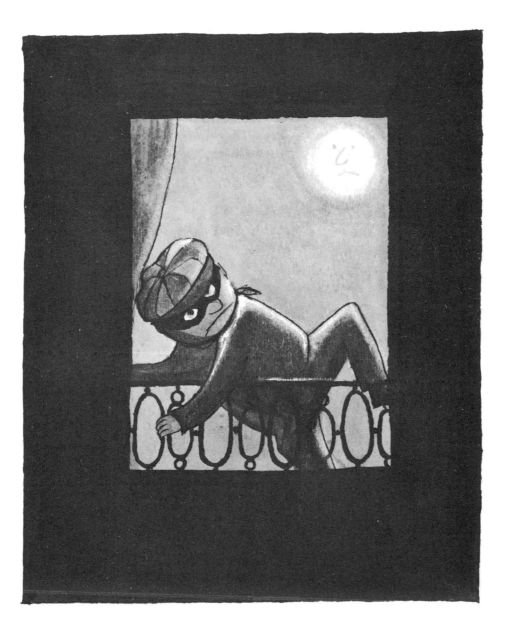

That very night the burglar broke into her apartment.

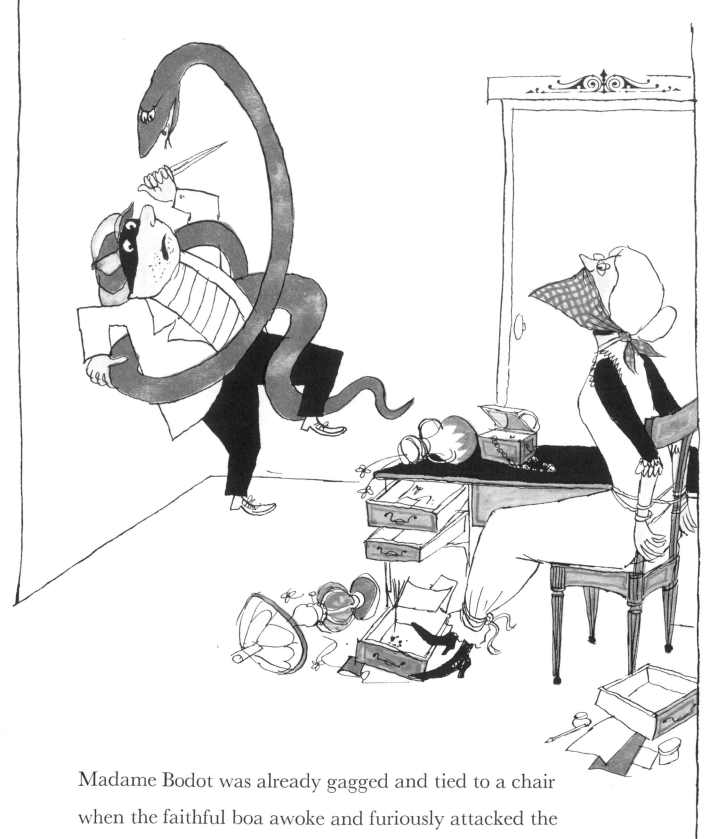

Madame Bodot was already gagged and tied to a chair
when the faithful boa awoke and furiously attacked the
28   burglar. The villain's terrified shrieks awoke the neighbors.

Crictor remained coiled around him until the police arrived.

For his bravery a nice medal was awarded to the heroic snake.

Crictor even inspired the local sculptor to make a statue in his honor.

And the city dedicated a park to him.

Loved and respected by the entire village,

Crictor lived a long and happy life.

The End